MAGIC
BONE

BROADWAY DOGGIE

For Ian and Mandy, native New Yorkers
no matter where they may roam—NK

For Oscar—SB

GROSSET & DUNLAP
Penguin Young Readers Group
An Imprint of Penguin Random House LLC

If you purchased this book without a cover, you should be aware that this book is
stolen property. It was reported as "unsold and destroyed" to the publisher, and neither
the author nor the publisher has received any payment for this "stripped book."

Penguin supports copyright. Copyright fuels creativity, encourages diverse voices,
promotes free speech, and creates a vibrant culture. Thank you for buying an
authorized edition of this book and for complying with copyright laws by not
reproducing, scanning, or distributing any part of it in any form without permission.
You are supporting writers and allowing Penguin to continue to publish
books for every reader.

The publisher does not have any control over and does not assume any responsibility
for author or third-party websites or their content.

Text copyright © 2016 by Nancy Krulik. Illustrations copyright © 2016 by
Sebastien Braun. All rights reserved. Published by Grosset & Dunlap, an imprint
of Penguin Random House LLC, 345 Hudson Street, New York, New York 10014.
GROSSET & DUNLAP is a trademark of Penguin Random House LLC.
Printed in the USA.

Library of Congress Cataloging-in-Publication Data is available.

ISBN 978-0-448-48875-2   10 9 8 7 6 5 4 3

MAGIC BONE

BROADWAY DOGGIE

by Nancy Krulik
illustrated by Sebastien Braun

Grosset & Dunlap
An Imprint of Penguin Random House

CHAPTER 1

"Sparky, sit."

I don't know many two-leg words, but I do know that one. So I push my bottom down onto the cold snow.

"Good dog," Josh says.

I smile. Those are two of my favorite two-leg words.

Josh lowers his paw. "Lie down."

I drop down onto my belly.

Josh flips his paw over. "Roll over."

I start to roll . . .

Plunk! Something hard lands on my head.

"Ow!" I bark.

Plink.

There's another.

Plunk.

And another. Those hard things hurt.

I look up.

Two squirrels are sitting on a tree branch. They are staring down at me.

Hee, hee, hee. And laughing.

"What's so funny?" I bark.

Plink. Plunk. Plink. Plunk.

The squirrels drop a *whole bunch* of hard round things on my head.

Hee, hee, hee.

"Stop throwing the hard round things!" I bark. "Stop laughing!"

Plink. Plunk. Plink.

"Ow!"

Grrr. The squirrels are all the way up in the tree. I could stop them if I could reach them. So I jump high. My paws claw at the tree.

"Sparky, DOWN!"

Suddenly, I hear Josh. I know what *down* means.

I stop jumping.

"Good dog," Josh says.

Plink. Plunk.

"OW!" I bark.

I am so mad, I forget what Josh said. I jump up and scratch the tree again.

"Sparky. Stay!" Josh says.

I know what *stay* means. I stand very, very still.

The squirrels get quiet. I think they are staying, too.

Josh twirls his paw around in a circle. "Twirl," he says.

I stand on my hind legs and turn in a circle. The squirrels don't. They don't know what *twirl* means.

Dogs are smarter than squirrels.

"Good dog." Josh pets me on the head.

"You want to do more tricks, Josh?" I bark. I love doing tricks. They make Josh smile.

But Josh doesn't want to do more tricks. He walks across the yard and opens the gate. I start to follow him.

"Sparky, stay!" Josh says.

I stay.

Now I can hear Josh's big metal machine with the four round paws. At first the sound is loud. Then it gets softer and softer, until it sounds far away.

Josh is gone. I'm all alone.

Plink. Plunk.

"Ouch!"

Well, not *all* alone. Those squirrels are still in the tree.

"Come down!" I say. "Play fair!"

I think the squirrels might understand, because they slide down the tree!

Then they start to run.

The squirrels want to play chase!

"Ready or not, here I come!" I start to chase them through my snowy yard.

The squirrels are fast. They climb onto the top of my fence. Then they leap over to the other side.

I can't get them there. Our game is over.

Now I'm really alone in my yard, with nothing to do.

Wait! There *is* something I can do. I can dig. I love digging.

I run over to where Josh's flowers are when there isn't snow in our yard. And I begin to dig.

Diggety, dig, dig. Lots of snow flies everywhere.

Diggety, dig, dig. The dirt under the snow flies all around, too. I am digging a really big hole.

Diggety, dig . . . WOW! What's this?

I found something buried deep in the dirt. It's a bone! A bright, sparkly, beautiful bone.

"Hello, bone!" I bark.

The bone doesn't answer. Bones can't bark.

Sniffety, sniff, sniff. The bone smells so meaty. I just have to take a bite.

Chomp.

Wiggle, waggle, whew. I feel dizzy—like my insides are spinning all around—but my outsides are standing still. Stars are twinkling in front of my eyes—even though it's daytime! All around me I smell food— fried chicken, salmon, roast beef. But there isn't any food in sight.

Kaboom! Kaboom! Kaboom!

CHAPTER 2

Where am I?

There's snow on the ground. Just like at my house.

There are trees here. Lots of trees. But none of them are *my* tree.

There are also a lot of two-legs walking around. But none of them are *my* two-leg.

I'm not in my yard anymore. I'm somewhere else. How did I get here?

Then I remember the yummy, meaty bone in my mouth. It's not just any bone. It's a *magic* bone. And it *kabooms* me places!

The first time I took a bite of my magic bone, it took me all the way to London, England. London was fun—and *yummy, yum, yum.* You wouldn't believe the snacks the two-legs there leave on the floor for dogs like me. Sausages, cheese, fish, and *chips.* That's what the dogs in London call fries.

And then another time my bone took me to Zermatt, Switzerland. That place has a lot more snow than here. And hot, yummy cheese called *fondue.*

But Zermatt was scary. I got caught in a big snowstorm. I didn't know if I would ever get back to my house again!

I want to make sure I can get back to my house today. So I have to hide my magic bone. I can't risk another dog finding it. Because my magic bone doesn't just *kaboom* me to faraway places. It *kabooms* me back home again, too.

I look around to see if there are any other dogs around, watching me. I don't see any. Just two-legs.

That's great. Because if a dog knew where my bone was, he might

diggety, dig, dig it up. But two-legs
don't really like digging.

I will bury my bone right next
to this giant water bowl. There's a
two-leg standing in the middle of the
water bowl. At least I think it's a two-
leg. It has wings on its back.

I have never seen a two-leg with
wings before.

The two-leg isn't moving. I wonder

if this two-leg is a statue two-leg. I know all about statues. I saw them when my magic bone *kaboomed* me to Rome.

I don't have time to figure out if this two-leg is real or a statue. I have to bury my bone before another dog sees me with it.

Diggety, dig, dig. Diggety, dig, dig.

I am making a huge hole in the cold, hard dirt. Quickly, I drop my bone in the big hole. Then I *pushity, push, push* the dirt back over my bone. No one will find it now.

Chitter-chatter.

I look over and see two squirrels by a tree. They look just like the squirrels from my yard.

I wonder if my bone has *kaboomed*

the squirrels from my yard to this place with me.

No. My magic bone only *kabooms* me. These must be different squirrels.

The squirrels start to run. They want to play chase.

"Ready or not, here I come," I bark. I start to chase after those squirrels. I run and run. Until . . .

Sniffety, sniff, sniff. My nose smells something yummy.

Grumble, rumble. That's my tummy talking. I know what it's saying. It wants to taste what my nose smells.

So I stop chasing the squirrels. Instead, I follow my nose. The good-smelling stuff is over by those stairs.

Sniffety, sniff, sniff. I'm getting closer.

Yum! There it is. A yummy smelling—

"Yo! That's *my* hot pretzel!"

I hear a dog yelling to me. I turn around to look at him.

Wiggle, waggle . . . uh-oh. That's a big dog. He's some sort of mixed-breed—with huge teeth.

"But it was just lying h-here," I tell him nervously.

"I was watching a little two-leg try and eat it. I knew he'd drop it. And he did. I was on my way over to pick up the scraps when you showed up."

"I'm s-sorry," I tell the big, scary dog. "If you want the pretzel, you can have it."

"We can share it," he suggests. "There's plenty to go around."

Maybe this dog isn't so scary after all! "Thanks!" I take a bite. "Yum!"

The mixed-breed takes a bite, too. "You're new around here, huh?" he says.

"Yes," I say. "I just got here."

"Where ya from?" he asks.

"Josh's house," I answer.

"You lived in a house? That must have been a sweet deal. Why did you leave?"

I don't want to tell him about my magic bone. So I just say, "I want to explore for a while. I'll go home later."

"You're gonna explore the Big Apple, huh?" the mixed-breed says.

"The Big Apple?" I look around. I don't see apples anywhere. "Why would a place be called a big apple if there aren't any apples?"

"That's just a nickname for New York City," he explains. He looks me up and down. "I don't know. You look a little too wimpy to hang out on these streets alone."

"I'm not wimpy," I say. Then I pause. "What does *wimpy* mean?"

The mixed-breed laughs. "Good thing you met me," he says. "I've spent my whole life in New York City. I'll show ya around. My name's Barney. What's yours?"

"Sparky."

"Well, Sparky, the first thing you should know is that not everybody in New York City is nice like me. This is the greatest city in the world. But there are some mean characters on the streets. They don't like to share their scraps—or anything."

"Speaking of scraps," I say. "Can I have the rest of that pretzel?"

"Sure," Barney says. "I already ate a hot dog anyhow."

Gulp. "You ate a dog?" I back away nervously.

The big dog laughs. "Not a dog like us," he explains. "A *hot dog*. It's like a skinny sausage. It doesn't have fur or a tail or anything."

Phew.

"There are a lot of hot-dog carts here in Central Park," he tells me. "So if you want to try a real New York hot dog—"

Coo . . . coo . . . coo.

"Look out," Barney says. "Here comes trouble."

CHAPTER 3

Coo . . . coo . . . coo.

A whole flock of gray birds surrounds us. A few of them start pecking at the pretzel on the ground.

"Get away from that pretzel, you flying rats," Barney barks angrily.

"Rats?" I ask. I don't understand. "Do New York rats have wings?"

Barney laughs. "Nah. But rats are a pain in the neck, just like pigeons."

I guess these gray birds are called pigeons.

"I said *get away*," Barney growls

to the pigeons. He bares his big teeth.
"And I meant it."

The birds stop pecking at the pretzel. They fly away.

Wow. Barney is one tough dog!

"That was awesome," I tell him. I start to take a bite of the pretzel.

Coo . . . coo . . . COOOOOO.

Uh-oh. The pigeons are back. And now there are more of them. *Lots* more.

"Looks like they brought a whole pigeon army," Barney grumbles as he starts to walk away. "No point arguing with the Ferocious Flyers over a pretzel scrap."

"Ferocious Flyers?" I ask.

"That's just what I call those pigeons," Barney says. "They'll do anything to get what they want. Squawk at you. Peck at you. Or *worse.*"

"Worse?" I repeat nervously.

"Anyway, come on," Barney says. "I know a great place to get scraps."

Wiggle, waggle, whoopee! I love scraps!

"Is it fun living in a house?" Barney asks me as we walk out of the park.

"Sure. Josh plays with me. And feeds me. And pets me." I stop for a minute. "Did you ever live in a house?"

"Nah," Barney says. "I'm a street dog. I don't want to live in a house. I

have a bigger dream. I want to be an actor on Broadway."

"A *what* on *where*?" I ask him.

"I want to act," Barney says. "In a Broadway theater."

I still have no idea what he's talking about.

"I want to do tricks in front of two-legs every night," Barney explains. "That's what Broadway show dogs do."

"Is it fun?" I ask.

"Oh yeah," Barney says. "I know this dog, Sandy, who acts in a show. He makes hundreds of two-legs happy every night. He's got a warm bed and lots of yummy snacks, too. That's how they treat stars in New York."

Now I understand why Barney wants to act. I love making Josh happy. And I love eating treats in bed.

Barney stops. "Here's one of those hot dogs I was telling you about," he says. "This one's still wrapped in its bun!"

Sniffety, sniff, sniff. That smells good. I open my mouth to take a bite and . . . OUCH!

I feel something peck me on the rear end.

The Ferocious Flyers are back. Now they want our hot dog.

Suddenly I feel something wet and gooey drop on my back. I turn my head as far as I can, but I can't see what it is.

"What's on my back?" I ask Barney.

"I told you pigeons fight dirty," Barney says. "One of them just pooped on you."

"That *is* dirty," I say. I flip over on the sidewalk and try to scratch off the bird poop.

"One of them got me, too," Barney says. "I need to go somewhere they can't go for a while."

"How are you going to do that?" I ask. "There are pigeons everywhere."

"Pigeons aren't allowed in any building in New York City," Barney says. "So I'm going in there." He uses his snout to point to a building straight ahead.

Barney starts climbing a big flight of stairs.

I don't want to be left alone with dirty-fighting birds.

"Wait up!" I shout to Barney. "I'm right behind you!"

CHAPTER 4

Barney zooms through an open door. He zigzags between a big crowd of two-legs who are all going through the door at once.

I follow right behind him. *Zig. Zag.*

There are lots of two-legs inside here. But they don't notice me. That's because they're all looking up.

I wonder what they're looking at.

I look up, too. *Wiggle, waggle, wow!* Those are the biggest bones I've ever seen!

"I'd like to take one of *those* home," I tell Barney.

Barney shakes his head. "You can't swipe a dinosaur bone," he says. "Those bones belong to the Museum of Natural History. If you took one, you'd be as bad as those Ferocious Flyers that are always stealing my scraps."

I didn't think of it like that.

"Uh-oh," Barney says suddenly.

"The Ferocious Flyers followed us?" I look around.

"Worse," Barney says. "It's the museum guards. We were able to sneak in with that crowd. But now they've spotted us."

"So what?" I say. "We're not pigeons. We can be inside here."

"Not exactly," Barney says slowly.

Uh-oh.

"You lied to me?" I ask.

"No," Barney says. "Pigeons aren't allowed inside *anywhere*. Dogs are allowed in some buildings. Just not this one."

The museum guards are getting closer. They look mad enough to throw Barney and me in a pound. *If they can catch us.*

"Let's make a run for it," I suggest.

"We can't," Barney says. "There's a guard at the door. And look at all these two-legs. Any one of them could catch us."

Gulp. What are we going to do?

Wait a minute. I have an idea.

"Stand still," I tell Barney. "Try

to look like one of these bony guys. Maybe the guards will think we belong here."

"That won't work," Barney says.

"It worked for me in Zermatt," I say. "I looked just like one of their ice statues. The two-legs didn't know the difference."

"But—" Barney begins.

"Do you have a better idea?" I ask him.

Barney doesn't answer. Instead he stands on his hind legs and tries to look like a dinosaur.

I do the same thing.

The guards come running. They go right past us.

Wiggle, waggle, woo-hoo! My trick worked!

Or maybe not. The guards turn around. They stare at Barney and me.

"They've spotted us," Barney says. "We gotta scram!"

"Where to?" I ask.

"You run to one side. I'll run to the other," Barney says. "We'll confuse them. They won't know which way to look."

That makes sense. Besides, it's

not like there's any other choice.

Zippity, zip, zoom! I run across the room!

Two-legs leap out of the way as I run. They don't want to get knocked over by a *zippity, zip, zooming* sheepdog puppy.

A guard is chasing right behind me. He is shouting. I don't understand what he's saying.

But I know what he wants to do. He wants to grab me. His paws are stretched out wide.

He won't grab *me*! No way!

"Come on, paws," I bark. "Run faster."

My paws speak dog. They run fast. Faster. *Fastest!*

I hurry past the guard at the door.

Down the stairs.

And out onto the street. *Whee!* I'm free.

But I don't see Barney anywhere. Oh no! Did the guard catch him?

I look up at the door. There's Barney. He's barking wildly.

"You better get out of my way, guard!" Barney barks.

The guard must speak dog, because he moves away and lets Barney go. He looks scared of the big barking dog in front of him.

"We made it!" I shout happily as Barney races down the steps. "We got away!"

"We sure did!" Barney exclaims.

But not for long. Just then I see a group of two-legs racing down the stairs. They run faster when they spot Barney and me.

"I knew it wouldn't be long before those guards came looking for us," Barney groans.

"What are we going to do?" I ask nervously.

"There's only one thing *to* do," Barney says. "Get out of here!"

42

CHAPTER 5

Run. Run. Run.

My heart is *thumpety, thump, thumping.* My paws are hurting.

"Can we stop now?" I ask Barney.

"We should probably get a little farther away from the museum," he answers. Then he looks at me. "You seem kinda tired, kid."

"I am," I admit. "It's hard to run on this hard, cold ground."

"Then let's catch a cab," Barney says.

Huh?

"Is that like catching a ball?" I ask him.

Barney laughs. "Not exactly," he says. He looks around. "Look, there's a cab now."

The next thing I know, Barney is jumping into a big metal machine with round paws.

So I jump in, too. A moment later, the machine starts moving slowly and quietly through the streets of New York City.

"I've never been in a metal machine like this one," I tell Barney. "Josh's machine makes a *vroom-vroom* noise when it moves. But this one doesn't."

"This is a different kind of metal machine," Barney says. "It's very quiet. The two-leg in the front has to move his legs up and down to make it go."

"That seems like a lot of work," I say. "Doesn't he get tired?"

"I don't know," Barney admits. "At least *we're* not getting tired."

That's true. Barney and I aren't doing anything. We're just riding along the streets of New York.

"Keep your head under the blanket," Barney warns me. "If the two-leg up front sees us, he'll throw us out."

"But I want to see New York," I tell him.

"Don't worry, kid, you will," Barney assures me. "You're with the best tour guide in the city—me."

Suddenly the metal machine stops. Someone whips off the blanket.

There are two two-legs standing there. They sure look surprised.

I guess they didn't expect to see dogs hidden under the blanket.

The two-leg in the front of the metal machine turns around. He starts to yell.

"Time to leave," Barney says.

Barney leaps out of the metal machine. So do I.

I follow him down some stairs. Barney runs fast. It is hard to keep up with him.

I'm *zoomity, zoom, zooming* down the stairs. My paws are moving fast. Fast. Faster . . . *WHOA!*

This ground is slippery-slidey.

Whoosh . . . I slide across the ground on my belly! *Wiggle, waggle, yikes!* The ground is cold!

My legs try to stand up. But my paws keep slipping out from under me. *Whoaaa!* I'm sliding all over the place.

Two-legs leap out of the way as I slide.

Bang! I slide right into a wall. That hurt.

I look up. There's Barney. But he's not slipping. Or sliding. He's moving around in circles. Kind of like some of the two-legs are doing.

Now he's walking . . . backward! One of the two-legs is walking with him.

"How do you do that?" I bark to Barney.

Barney doesn't answer. He just walks around in a circle again.

A group of two-legs are watching Barney. They are hitting their paws together. And smiling. Barney is making all the two-legs happy.

Well, *almost* all the two-legs. There's a group of angry-looking two-legs running down the stairs. They race onto the slippery-slidey cold ground and start to chase Barney and me.

"Show's over, Sparky," Barney calls to me. "We gotta get out of here!"

Barney runs across the slippery-slidey ground and races up the stairs. It seems easy for him.

But it's not easy for me. I run two steps. Then I fall.

"Hurry, Sparky!" Barney shouts. "You don't want to be taken to the pound!"

"I'm trying," I bark. But it's hard
to hurry when you keep falling.
Run. Fall.
Run. Fall.

The two-legs are getting closer.
Run. Fall. Run.
Finally, I reach the stairs.
"Follow me!" Barney shouts as I
run up the stairs.

A moment later, we are all alone on a small, narrow street. Just me and Barney.

"That was a close one," Barney says.

I try to catch my breath.

"That ground sure was slippery," I say finally. "I couldn't walk. But you were amazing."

Barney smiles. "Thanks, pal," he says.

"You made those two-legs really happy," I tell him. "Was that acting?"

Barney shakes his head. "Nah," he says. "That was skating."

All of a sudden my teeth start moving up and down. Only I'm not eating. Or talking. I'm just cold.

"I wish I had that blanket now,"

I tell Barney.

"Yeah, it's pretty chilly out. We should—"

Suddenly Barney stops talking. His ears perk up.

"Uh-oh," he says. "The two-legs are coming this way. We gotta find a better place to hide."

"But this is a good hiding place," I tell him. "We're the only ones here."

"That's what makes it a rotten hiding place," Barney explains. "In New York, the best place to hide is in a crowd. And I know where we can find the biggest crowds of all!"

CHAPTER 6

There are two-legs in front of me.

There are two-legs behind me.

There are two-legs all around me.

I've never seen so many two-legs. There are so many, I can barely move. It's kind of scary.

"Welcome to Times Square, Sparky," Barney says. "Isn't it beautiful?"

I can't see if it's beautiful. All I can see are legs.

"Come on," Barney says. "I want to show you something special."

Barney starts to walk, so I do, too. I stay really, really close to him. My nose is practically touching his tail. I don't want to get lost in this crowd.

Suddenly, Barney stops walking. He looks up. "Isn't this amazing?" he asks me.

I look up. But I don't see anything amazing. "It's just a building," I say.

Barney stares at me. He seems surprised. "It's not just *any* building," he tells me. "It's a Broadway theater."

Oh. Now I get it.

"Every visitor to New York City should go see a Broadway theater," Barney says proudly.

"What does it look like on the inside?" I ask him.

Barney shrugs. "I don't know. I've

never been *inside*. But I will be. One day, two-legs will come from all over to watch me do my tricks. They will cheer when I sit. And lie down. And dance on my hind legs. And roll over."

I watch as Barney sits. And lies down. And dances. And rolls over.

I wonder if Barney had to go to

school to learn those tricks. That's where I learned them.

A crowd of two-legs walks by. Barney leaps up on his hind legs and twirls around. They don't even notice. They're too busy walking by.

Barney looks sad.

"You would have made them smile if we were inside," I say. "It is too cold out here for *anyone* to be happy."

"Yeah, I guess," Barney agrees. "It is cold. Come on. I'll show you a great place to warm up."

Barney and I go around the corner.

I sure hope he's taking me to a nice warm house. Maybe one with a comfy couch. And some yummy treats. That would be perfect.

Barney stops in front of a building.

My tail starts to wag. It thinks we're going inside. That makes my tail very happy.

Barney plops down on top of some metal bars in the middle of the sidewalk.

"Aaaahhhh," Barney sighs. "My favorite grate."

My tail stops wagging. "It doesn't look so *great* to me," I say.

Barney gives me a funny look. Then he laughs.

"No, it's a *grate*. A break in the sidewalk. There's hot air coming up from down there."

I guess it's worth a try. I am awfully cold.

Slowly, I sit down on the metal

bars. Hot air hits me right on the rear end.

"This is nice," I say.

"Told ya," Barney says. "And the best part is, from here we can see everything going on in Times Square."

There sure is a lot going on. There are lots of metal machines with round paws. And two-legs are *zoomity, zoom, zooming* all around. And . . .

Coo . . . coo . . . coo.

Pigeons! The Ferocious Flyers are back!

Coo . . . coo . . . coo.

"What do they want now?" I ask Barney.

"I think they want to warm up over this grate," Barney says. "But that's not happening. We were here first."

Barney sits up tall. "Get outta here," he growls at the pigeons. "Go find your own warm grate. Maybe over in Jersey."

When Barney growls, he sounds really scary.

But I don't think the Ferocious Flyers are scared. Because a whole bunch more of them are flying over us now. There are so many pigeons, I can barely see the sky.

"Hey!" I shout as I jump out of the way of a big blob of falling bird poop. "That's not nice!"

Coo . . . coo . . . coo.

The pigeons sound like they are laughing at me. Just like the squirrels in my yard.

Grrr.

"It's easy for them to win a fight," I tell Barney. "They're way up there where we can't reach them. If I could fly, I'd show them."

Barney starts to smile. "That's a great idea," he says.

"What are you talking about?" I ask him. "Dogs can't fly."

"No," Barney admits. "But we can do the next best thing!"

CHAPTER 7

Uh-oh.

Barney and I have just walked into a big room. The door has shut, tight. We're locked in here with a whole bunch of two-legs. But that's not the uh-oh part.

The uh-oh part is that the room is moving. It's going up, up, up.

Barney and I are locked in a moving room with a bunch of two-leg strangers.

The two-leg strangers don't look too happy to be locked in here with us, either. They've all moved to one corner of the room. They're pointing at us. And they aren't smiling.

"What's going on?" I ask Barney nervously.

"You said you wanted to fly," Barney tells me. "This is as close as it gets."

"I didn't say I wanted to fly," I remind him. "I said *if* I could fly."

"Same thing," Barney says. "When we get out of here, we're going to be high up in the sky. Just like the Ferocious Flyers."

Gulp. I've been high up before. At the top of the Washington Monument in Washington, DC. It was really scary up there.

Just then, the room stops moving

up, up, up. The door opens. The two-legs run out. They can't get away from us fast enough.

"Come on, Sparky," Barney says. "You're gonna love this."

I follow Barney out of the room. *Whoosh!* A blast of cold air hits me right in the face.

"I-I-I want to go back in the room that moves up, up, up," I tell Barney. "I want it to take me down, down, down."

"Come on, Sparky. Just check this out," Barney urges.

I walk over to where Barney is standing. I look out. Then I look down . . .

Uh-oh. I shouldn't have done that. Now I know how far away the ground is. *Very* far away.

The metal machines with four round paws are so far away, they look like chew toys. And the two-legs are so tiny, they look like I could swallow them up in one gulp.

Out there in the distance, I see one two-leg. She looks bigger than the others. She's a funny green color. And she's standing right in the middle of a giant bowl of water.

"What kind of two-leg—?" I start.

But I don't get to finish my question. Because just then, I hear a lot of shouting.

It's two-leg shouting, so I can't understand what they're saying. But I get the feeling that they're yelling at Barney and me.

"We gotta get out of here," Barney says. "Those could be dogcatchers."

"D-d-dogcatchers?" I ask Barney nervously.

"Dogs aren't really allowed on the observation deck of the Empire State Building," Barney says.

Now he tells me.

Coo . . . coo . . . coo.

As if things weren't bad enough, the Ferocious Flyers have arrived.

"Get out of here," Barney growls

at the birds, "before I bite off your tail feathers."

That scares those birds away real fast. They fly off.

"The Ferocious Flyers are such chickens," Barney says with a laugh.

"I thought they were pigeons?" I say.

Barney gives me a look.

The dogcatchers aren't afraid of Barney's bark. They're still coming right for us.

I run to the room that moved up, up, up. But the door is shut. We can't escape that way.

"Let's go, Sparky," Barney tells me. "We gotta take the stairs."

"Stairs?" I ask him. "From all the way up here?"

"We have no choice," Barney says. He starts running down the stairs. I follow close behind.

Thump, thump. Thump, thump.

Uh-oh. Now I can hear two-legs running down the stairs behind us. So I run faster. So does Barney.

"I don't get why dogs aren't allowed in this building, but pigeons are," I say as we run. "Pigeons are mean. They don't cuddle with two-legs. They don't do tricks."

"I know," Barney agrees. "Pigeons are the ones that should be put in pounds!"

Barney and I have been running down a lot of stairs. My paws hurt. My tongue is hanging out of my mouth.

I'm running down the stairs so fast, my fur flies in my eyes. I can't see a thing. But I keep running. Fast. Faster. *Fastest.*

Thud.

Wiggle, waggle, uh-oh!

I run right into a two-leg.

The two-leg wraps his paws around my middle. He lifts me off the ground.

"Barney! Help!" I bark as loud as I can.

Barney doesn't answer.

I wiggle and squiggle. "Let go of me, two-leg!" I bark.

But the two-leg holds me tighter. I can't break free. This is *baddy, bad, bad.*

"Don't take me to the pound!" I bark to the two-leg. "Please don't!"

CHAPTER 8

"What is this place?" I ask.

The strong two-leg has dropped me in a huge room full of dogs. Big dogs. Little dogs. Puppies. Grown-up dogs.

Dogs are everywhere.

Some are resting on pillows.

Some are chewing toys.

Some are licking their paws.

Everywhere I look, there's another dog.

A furry mixed breed looks up at me. "You're at a shelter," she tells me.

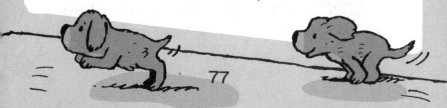

"A what?" I ask her.

"An animal shelter," a little bouncy Chihuahua says. "A place where four-legs that don't have two-legs live."

"You mean like a pound?" I ask nervously.

"I don't know what a pound is," the mixed breed admits. She gives me a smile. "Relax, puppy. It's not so scary here. Most of the dogs that come through are really nice. And they keep the cats in a different room."

"We're all here waiting for the same thing—a two-leg to fall in love with us and take us to a *fur-ever* home," a sad-eyed basset hound adds.

"But I already have a *fur-ever* home," I tell them. "With Josh."

"Not anymore," the Chihuahua

says. "This is your home—at least for now. But don't worry. It's nice and warm here. And you get food. This place has everything a dog needs."

That's not true. I need Josh.

My tail droops. So do my ears. They are very sad to be in the shelter.

"I want to go home!" I cry out.

"Quiet down," the mixed breed says gently. "Two-legs don't like dogs that bark too loudly."

That's not true, either. Josh likes when I bark at the door when he gets home.

Maybe Josh is different than other two-legs. Maybe other two-legs don't like barking the way Josh does.

That could be. Because there is only one Josh. And I want to go home and be with him.

Suddenly the Chihuahua starts bouncing up and down. "Someone's coming! Someone's coming!" he yips excitedly.

The door opens. A group of two-legs walks into the room.

"Pick me! Pick me!" the Chihuahua yips as he bounces.

"I'm a good dog," the mixed breed barks. "You'd like me—even if my fur sheds on your carpet."

"I need a buddy," the basset hound howls. "You want to be my buddy?"

I don't say anything. I do not want to go home with any of these two-legs. I want to go to *my* home.

One of the two-legs walks to the middle of the room. He turns his paw over and lifts it up.

The Chihuahua keeps bouncing up and down.

The mixed breed lies down.

The basset hound just stands there.

But I sit.

81

I can't help it. That's what I do every time a two-leg raises his paw like that.

Now the two-leg lowers his paw to the ground.

I lie down. Whenever I see a two-leg put his paw on the ground, I have to lie down. That's what I learned to do when I was in school.

The two-leg lifts his paw and twirls it around in a circle.

So I jump up onto my hind legs and twirl in a circle.

The other dogs stare at me.

"What's he doing?" the basset hound asks.

"Show-off," the Chihuahua yips.

"Speak!" the two-leg orders.

"I'm not showing off," I tell the

Chihuahua. "I can't help it. He's doing paw signals."

The two-leg gives me a big smile. He thinks I was barking because he said *speak*. But I was just talking to the other dogs.

Another two-leg comes over. He points to my collar.

The two-leg bends down to look at the little metal thing hanging from my collar. He flips it over.

He is looking for something. But I don't know what.

The next thing I know, the two-leg snaps a leash onto my collar. He hands the leash to the two-leg who knows paw signals.

The two-leg with the leash starts to lead me out of the room.

"Wow. I have to learn some of those paw signals," the basset hound howls.

"He got a two-leg on his very first day," the mixed breed says. "Amazing."

"Lucky guy," the Chihuahua yips.

I shake my head. I don't feel lucky. I just feel scared. And lonely.

And very, very sad.

CHAPTER 9

"I will not eat the treat," I tell myself. "I will not eat the treat."

A two-leg is holding a treat in front of my snout. But I don't eat it. I am too sad to eat anything.

Sniffety, sniff, sniff. The treat does smell yummy, though. Like peanut butter.

Peanut-butter treats are my favorite. Maybe it wouldn't hurt to try just one.

Chew, chew, chew.

The treat is really yummy. But it

doesn't make me feel any happier. I do not like being in this place.

The floor is made of hard wood. Bright lights are shining in my eyes. I can barely see. But I can tell that there are a lot of chairs. They look comfy and cozy.

But the two-legs are not sitting in the chairs. They are standing up here on the hard wood floor. I don't know why we all don't curl up in those comfy-cozy chairs.

The two-leg who took me out of the shelter walks over. He raises his hand up.

"Sit," he says.

My bottom flops down. I don't have to tell my bottom to sit. It just does.

The two-leg holds out his paw.

"Shake," he says.

My paw lifts itself off the ground. The two-leg shakes my paw up and down.

Then the two-leg puts his paw on the ground.

"Lie down," he says.

My legs bend. My belly touches the floor.

The two-leg pulls his hand back.

"Stand up," he says.

My legs straighten. I stand up.

The two-leg twirls his paw around and around.

"Twirl," he says.

I jump up onto my hind legs. I twirl in a circle. *Twirl. Twirl. Twirl.* I can't help myself.

"Good dog," the two-leg says. He gives me a peanut-butter treat.

Then he starts the whole thing all over again.

Sit. Shake. Lie down. Stand up. Twirl.

Sit. Shake. Lie down. Stand up. Twirl.

Now all the two-legs in this big room are smiling.

They hit their paws together.

They say, "Good dog."

I don't know why they think it is such a big deal. I understand a lot of two-leg words. What I don't understand is why two-legs never want to learn any *dog* words.

The two-leg who took me out of the shelter holds his hand up. Here we go again.

Sit. Shake. Lie down. Stand up. Twirl.

I am getting very tired of doing tricks. I want to go back to the park and dig up my magic bone. One chomp, and it will *kaboom* me right home.

But I can't dig up my bone if I'm stuck here.

There's only one thing to do. I am going to have to make a run for it!

I leap from the edge of the hard, wooden floor. I land right near the chairs below. Then I take off.

I can hear the two-legs yelling at me. I know they want me to stop. But I *can't*.

I don't have time to do any more tricks for them. I have to get home.

So I keep running. Fast. Faster. *Fastest*.

Wiggle, waggle, whee! Those two-legs won't catch me!

93

CHAPTER 10

"*Have you ever seen talent like this?*"

That's the first thing I hear when I get outside. It's definitely a dog talking.

I stop running and turn around. That's when I see Barney. He's sitting. And rolling over. And twirling on his hind legs.

"Come on, don't leave me waiting in the wings," he calls to a two-leg passing by. "Put me center stage!"

Barney sure is talking funny. What wings? Dogs don't have wings. Pigeons have wings. And that weird two-leg in the water bowl in the park.

"Barney!" I bark excitedly. "There you are."

My pal stops twirling. He looks over at me. Then he looks up at the building I just came out of.

"Were you in there?" he asks me.

I nod. "It was awful," I tell him. "Really bright lights. A hardwood floor and—"

"Some friend you are," Barney interrupts me. He sounds angry.

That's weird. Why would Barney be angry? He wasn't the one with the lights in his eyes. He wasn't the one who had to do the same tricks over and over. He wasn't the one who was in the scary shelter.

"Why are you mad at me?" I yell. "I should be mad at you. When that two-leg captured me, you didn't help. You just ran away!"

"I didn't just run away," Barney says. "I turned around, and you were gone. I looked all over the place for you. I asked all the dogs in the neighborhood. None of them saw you. I was really worried."

"Oh," I say. Now I feel bad for yelling at him. "I didn't know that."

"Besides, if I'd known that two-leg was going to put you in a Broadway show, *I* would have *jumped* into his arms!" Barney barks. "I'd have been glad to have him take me over you."

"He didn't put me in a show," I tell him. "He put me in a shelter. Then another two-leg took me to this place."

"This place is a real *Broadway theater!*" Barney shouts at me. "They are casting a brand-new show. You're gonna be a star, Sparky."

Oh no I'm not. I don't want to be a star. I just want to go home and be a puppy. *Josh's* puppy.

"That wasn't a show," I tell him. "You said there would be hundreds of two-legs watching when you act in a show. But there were only a few in there."

"That's just because that was a *rehearsal*," Barney says.

"A what?" I ask him.

"A rehearsal," he repeats. "When

actors practice their parts over and over until they know them. You have to learn your part before you can do a show."

"He did make me do the same tricks again and again," I say. "Sit. Shake. Lie down. Stand up. Twirl."

"Easy stuff," Barney huffs.

"Well, I'm not going to do any more tricks for them," I tell Barney. "I'm out of here."

"You can't just walk out on a Broadway show," Barney tells me. "Haven't you heard 'the show must go on'?"

"The show will have to go on without me," I tell him.

I start to leave. Then I see a group of two-legs running out of the theater.

One of them is the two-leg who made me do all those tricks.

Suddenly, I *thinkety, think* of a great idea!

"Now's your chance, Barney," I say. "Show them what you can do."

I run and hide behind a round metal can. I don't think the two-leg who made me do tricks can see me here. But I can see him through the holes in the can.

I can see Barney, too. He's doing tricks. Lots of them.

Sit. Shake. Lie down. Stand up. Twirl.

Barney adds a special kick with his back paw. It makes his twirl look fancy.

The two-legs all stare at

Barney. So Barney does the tricks all over again.

The two-legs hit their paws together. They smile.

The two-leg who made me do all those tricks holds out his paw. Barney sniffs it and takes a treat.

Then he starts to follow the two-legs into the theater.

Suddenly, he stops. He looks around. And then he barks.

"Thanks, Sparky!" he says. "I passed the audition. Look out, Broadway. Here I come!"

Wiggle, waggle, yippee! Finally Barney's dream is coming true. He is going to be a star!

Now it's my turn to get what *I* want.

Look out, Josh. Here I come!

CHAPTER 11

I look around. I do not see the park with the big water bowl anywhere. It must be very far away.

I am tired. All that sitting, shaking, and twirling has really worn me out.

But I am not going to let that stop me.

I stand on the side of the street. I wait for one of the funny quiet metal machines with round paws to come by. Then I jump inside, just like Barney showed me.

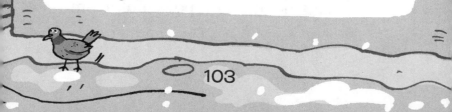

I hide under the blanket as the metal machine moves through the streets of New York. The two-leg in front does not know I am here. Neither do the Ferocious Flyers.

Every now and then I poke my head out of the blanket to look around.

All I see are buildings. And two-legs. And lots and lots of metal machines.

Uh-oh. What if this one doesn't know where the park is? What if I can't find my way back to my bone?

Sniffety, sniff, sniff.

Suddenly I smell something meaty—like a hot dog in a bun.

I sneak another peek out from

under the blanket. Now I see lots and lots of trees.

I've only seen that many trees in one place in New York City. The park!

I wait for the metal machine to stop. Then I leap out from under the blanket.

I *zoomity, zoom, zoom* across the snow-covered grass.

Finally, I reach the big water bowl near where I buried my bone. And then I start to dig.

Plink.

Plunk.

Hee, hee, hee.

I stop digging. I look up. There are two squirrels in a tree. They're laughing at me.

Plink.

Plunk.

And dropping hard things on my head.

I could chase those squirrels. I could show them who's boss.

But I won't. Because I want to get home.

So I start to dig again. Snow and dirt fly everywhere. And then . . .

There it is.

My magic bone! It's sitting in the middle of the big hole. Right where I left it.

Then I see something else lying in the snow. It looks like those big bony statues in the museum. Except this one is little.

Barney said I shouldn't take one of the giant bones because they belonged to the museum. But this little chew toy is lying here in the dirt. It doesn't belong to anyone.

So I clasp it between my paws. Then I open my mouth to bite down on my yummy magic bone.

Coo . . . coo . . . coo.

Uh-oh. The Ferocious Flyers have spotted me.

I don't speak pigeon. But I have a feeling the Ferocious Flyers want to peck at my magic bone. I don't blame them. It smells delicious.

But I'm not sharing.

"Good-bye, Ferocious Flyers!" I bark.

Then I bite down on my magic bone. *Chomp.*

Wiggle, waggle, whew. I feel dizzy—like my insides are spinning all around—but my outsides are standing still. Stars are twinkling in front of my eyes—even though it's daytime! All around me I smell food—fried chicken, salmon, roast beef. But there isn't any food in sight.

Kaboom! Kaboom! Kaboom!

Wiggle, waggle, whoopee! I see my tree! And my fence! And my house!

I am happy to be back in my yard, but it's cold out here. I want to go inside.

I drop my chew toy on the ground. I run over to where I found my bone before. Then I start to *diggety, dig, dig*. Dirt and snow fly everywhere.

Wow! That's a big hole.

I drop my bone in. Then I *pushity, push, push* the cold dirt back over my bone.

Vroom. Vroom. I hear a metal machine. And it's getting closer. That can only mean one thing.

JOSH IS HOME!

I scoop up my new chew toy. Then I *zoomity, zoom, zoom* into the house through my doggie door. I wait for Josh to open the big door.

My new chew toy drops out of my mouth. "Hi, Josh!" I bark at the big door. "Come inside!"

I think Josh might be starting to understand dog. Because the next thing I know, the door opens, and Josh comes inside.

"Josh!" I bark.

Josh pets me on the head. Then he looks down at the floor. He spots my new chew toy.

Josh gives me a funny look. I think he is wondering where the toy came from.

I wish I could tell him about the giant bones in the museum.

And about the mean old Ferocious Flyers.

And about my new friend Barney who is going to be a Broadway star.

But I can't. So instead I sit. And shake. And lie down. And stand. And twirl. Then I add a little kick. Just like Barney.

Josh smiles. He laughs. He hits his paws together.

I smile back at Josh. My tail wags.

COME
and
visit
New
York

NEW YORK

My tail and I love making Josh happy.

Barney may be acting in a Broadway show in New York City. But in this house, *I'm* the star.

Fun Facts about Sparky's Adventures in New York City

New York City

The city includes five separate boroughs, or areas where people live and work. They are called the Bronx, Brooklyn, Manhattan, Queens, and Staten Island. Sparky spent his time in the borough of Manhattan.

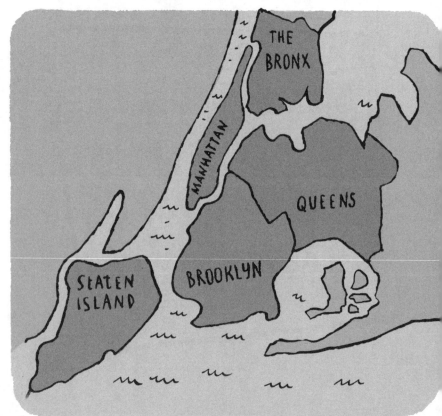

Central Park

This 843-acre park is one of the most popular places to visit in the world. About forty million people stop by each year. There are many things visitors can do in Central Park, including rowing boats, bird watching, picnicking, and taking a ride on a carousel.

American Museum of Natural History

This museum is made up of twenty-seven connected buildings and has forty-five exhibit halls. Throughout the museum are dioramas and other exhibits that show the way animals, plants, and people live. There is also a planetarium. The American Museum of Natural History is home to many dinosaur fossils, including a full-size *Tyrannosaurus rex*.

The Rink at Rockefeller Center

This ice-skating rink opened on Christmas Day in 1936. The rink is open to visitors from November to April every year and is one of the most popular tourist attractions in the city.

Times Square

Times Square is located at the intersection of Broadway and Seventh Avenue. It is sometimes called the Crossroads of the World because it is one of the busiest places anywhere. More than three hundred thousand people pass through Times Square *every day* to visit its restaurants, shops, hotels, and theaters.

Broadway Theaters

There are forty Broadway theaters in New York City. Each theater has more than five hundred seats. Most of them are located near Times Square. This part of Broadway is sometimes called the Great White Way because there are so many bright lights on the giant signs above the theaters.

The Empire State Building

This giant skyscraper has 103 floors. There are 73 elevators in the building. There are 1,860 steps from the street level to the 102nd floor. From observation decks on the 84th and 102nd floors, visitors can see almost all of Manhattan and beyond! There are so many businesses located in the Empire State Building that it has been given its own zip code—10118.

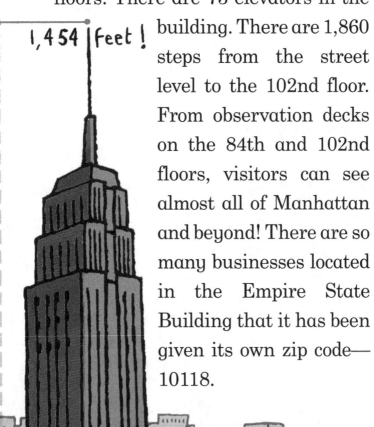

1,454 feet!

About the Author

Nancy Krulik is the author of more than 200 books for children and young adults, including three *New York Times* Best Sellers. She is best known for being the author and creator of several successful book series for children, including Katie Kazoo, Switcheroo; How I Survived Middle School; and George Brown, Class Clown. Nancy lives in Manhattan with her husband, composer Daniel Burwasser, and her crazy beagle mix, Josie, who manages to drag her along on many exciting adventures without ever leaving Central Park.

About the Illustrator

You could fill a whole attic with Seb's drawings! His collection includes some very early pieces made when he was four—there is even a series of drawings he did at the movies in the dark! When he isn't doodling, he likes to make toys and sculptures, as well as bows and arrows for his two boys, Oscar and Leo, and their numerous friends. Seb is French and lives in England.

His website is www.sebastienbraun.com.